MW01046068

Vipo Visits New York City

Why should you believe in yourself?

Ido Angel

ANIMATED STORYTIME
AV2 BY WEIGL
ADDED VALUE • AUDIO VISUAL

www.av2books.com

Go to www.av2books.com, and enter this book's unique code.

BOOK CODE

E297744

AV² by Weigl brings you media enhanced books that support active learning.

First Published by vipo

VipoLand Incorporated
32nd East Street No 3-32,
City of Panama,
Republic of Panama

Published by AV² by Weigl
350 5th Avenue, 59th Floor New York, NY 10118
Website: www.av2books.com

Library of Congress Control Number: 2015947863

ISBN: 978-1-4896-3917-2 (hardcover)
ISBN: 978-1-4896-3918-9 (single user eBook)
ISBN: 978-1-4896-3919-6 (multi-user eBook)

Editor: Katie Gillespie
Project Coordinator: Alexis Roumanis
Art Director: Terry Paulhus

Printed in the United States of America in Brainerd, Minnesota
1 2 3 4 5 6 7 8 9 0 19 18 17 16 15

082015
100715

MORAL OF THE STORY

For thousands of years, parents and teachers have used memorable stories called fables to teach simple moral lessons to children.

In the Vipo by AV² series, three friends travel to different countries around the world. They help people learn many important life lessons.

In *Vipo Visits New York City*, Vipo and his friends teach two cats to believe in themselves. The cats learn that everyone has something special to share.

This AV² media enhanced book comes alive with...

Animated Video
Watch a custom animated movie.

Try This!
Complete activities and hands-on experiments.

Key Words
Study vocabulary, and complete a matching word activity.

Quiz
Test your knowledge.

Why should you believe in yourself?

AV^2 Storytime Navigation

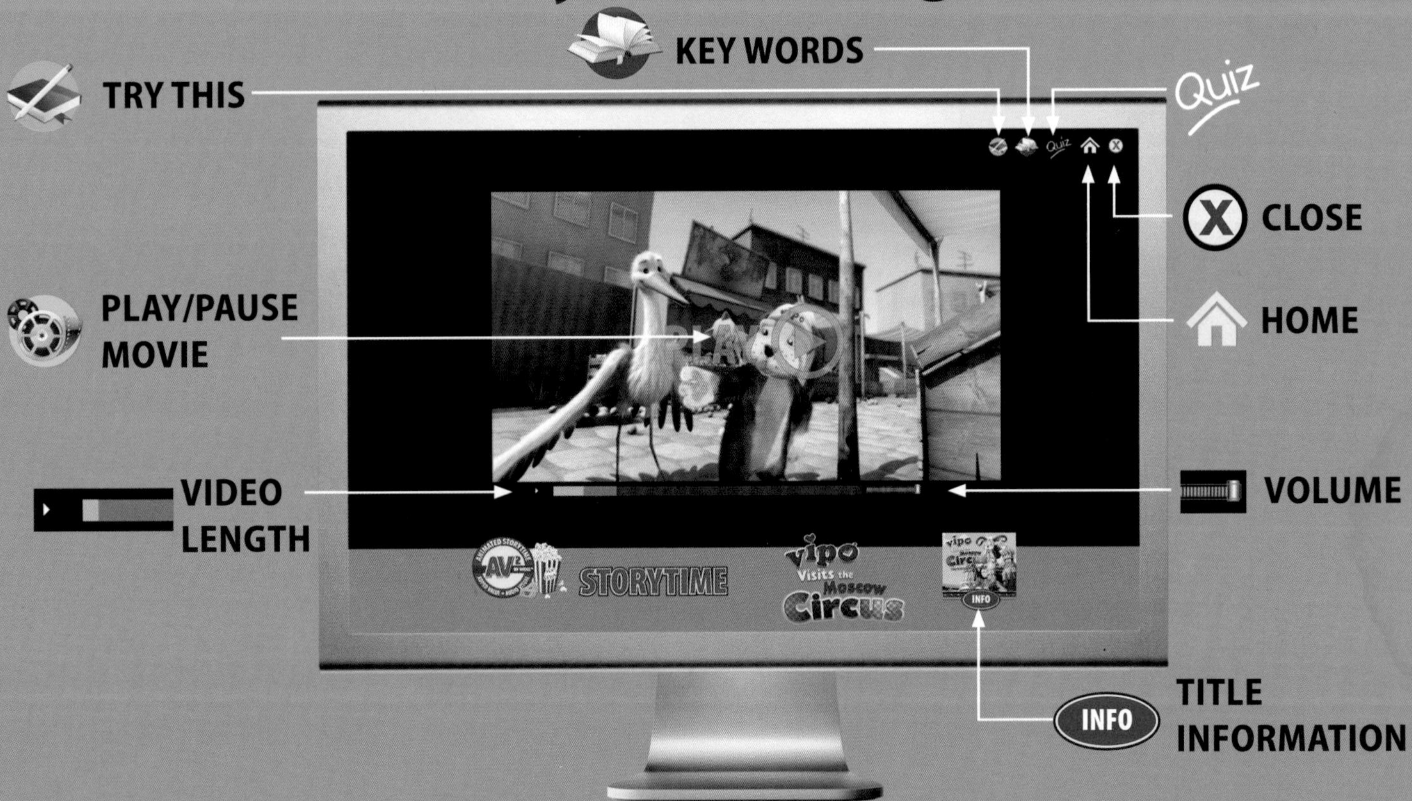

The Characters

Henry
I am a stork. I like going on adventures with Vipo. I am curious about the world.
Betty
I am a cat. I like to make friends with people from many different places. I like to help others.

The Story

One day, Vipo, Henry, and Betty were flying above New York City.

They landed at a busy train station next to two squirrels.

"Jimmy, help!" cried one of the squirrels. "It's a cat."

"Why are you scared of me?" asked Betty.

"Two cats are trying to steal our uncle's play," said Jenny.

"We're on our way to help him," said Jimmy.

"Why would cats want to steal a play?" asked Henry.
"We heard that the cats are making a new play," said Jenny.
"They want to steal our uncle's ideas," said Jimmy.
"We can take you to your uncle," said Henry.
"Jump on my back," said Vipo. "We will help him together."
The five of them flew out of the station.

Two cats were dancing to music at the train station.
They watched as Vipo flew off with the squirrels.
"Oliver, they're going to find Florence before we do," said the cat with the blue hat.
"Otis, they will lead us right to him," said Oliver.
"Then we'll be able to steal Florence's play," said Otis.
"Hurry! Let's follow them," cried Oliver.
The two cats ran after the squirrels.

The squirrels led Vipo to their uncle's theater.
When they knocked, a monkey opened the door.
"We are looking for Florence," said Vipo.
"I'm Florence. I'm wearing a monkey costume."

Florence took off his costume and hugged Jimmy and Jenny.
"Cats are trying to steal your play!" cried Jenny.
"I know," said Florence. "Let's go to the park and get some hot dogs to eat. Then, I'll tell you all about it."

Oliver and Otis watched them leave the theater.
"There he is!" cried Otis. "Let's grab him."
They followed the group, and could hear Florence talking.
"My play is only missing one thing," said Florence.
"What is it missing?" asked Henry.
"I don't know," said Florence. "That's why the play has taken so long to finish."
Suddenly, a rope landed around Jimmy.

"I've got him!" exclaimed Oliver.

Oliver and Otis pulled on the rope and grabbed Jimmy.

"You got the wrong one," cried Otis.

"It's too late," said Oliver. "We have to run!"

Oliver and Otis ran away with Jimmy in their arms.

"They took Jimmy into that house over there!" said Henry.
Florence stopped at the theater and put on a cat costume.
"This costume looks like their leader," said Florence.
They arrived at the cats' house.
"Wait by the window," said Florence.
Florence went inside, dressed in his cat costume.
"Can I see him?" asked Florence.
"See who?" replied Oliver.
"The squirrel you kidnapped," said Florence.

2
3

"Here he is," said Oliver, pointing to Jimmy.
Florence took off his costume.
"Follow me, Jimmy!" shouted Florence.
Florence and Jimmy jumped out of the window.
The others were there waiting for them.
"Quickly!" said Henry. "Let's run to the roof."
The two cats followed close behind.

The cats found Vipo's group on the roof.
"Why do you want Florence's play?" asked Betty.
"We don't know how to write a play," said Oliver.
"But we like to put on shows," Otis told them.
"Everyone has different talents," said Vipo.
"What are you two good at?" Florence asked.
"We like to dance," said Otis. "Watch!"
Otis and Oliver started dancing.

"That's just what my show is missing!" clapped Florence.
"Will you both dance in my play?"
"Yes!" cried Oliver. "We can work together."
"My play will be much better with you in it," said Florence.

Moral of the Story

You should always believe in yourself. Everyone has something special to share.

Vipo Visits New York City Quiz

1
Who did Vipo meet at the train station?

2
What were the cats doing at the train station?

3
Which costume did Uncle Florence wear first?

4
What did the group eat at the park?

5
Where did the group go to hide from the cats?

6
What was Uncle Florence's play missing?

Answers:

1. Jimmy and Jenny
2. They were following Jimmy and Jenny
3. A monkey costume
4. Hot dogs
5. The roof
6. Dancing

Check out www.av2books.com for your animated storytime media enhanced book!

1. Go to www.av2books.com
2. Enter book code **E297744**
3. Fuel your imagination online!

www.av2books.com

AV² Storytime Navigation

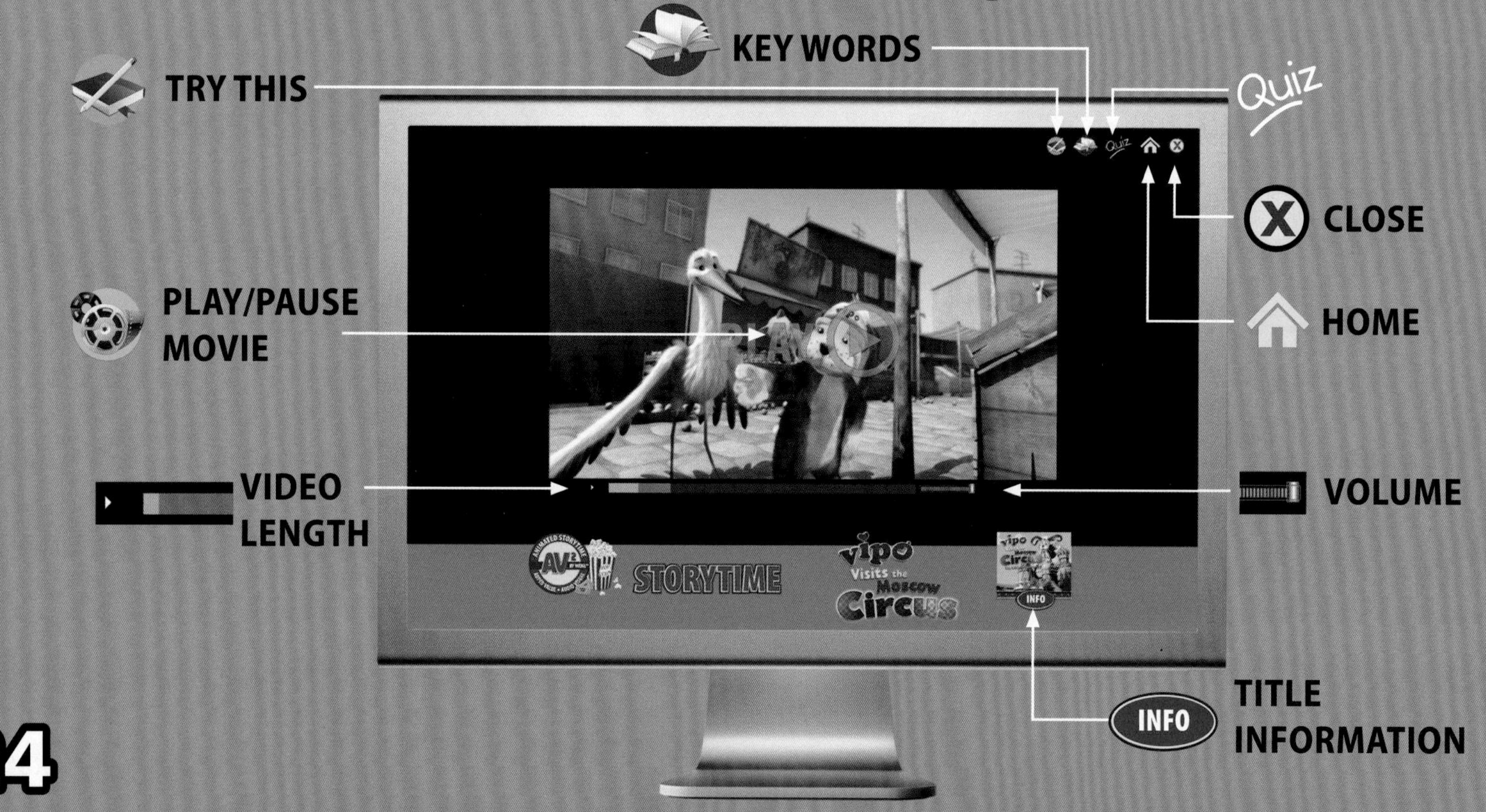